Science Matters
STARS

Jonathan Bocknek

WEIGL PUBLISHERS INC.

Published by Weigl Publishers Inc.
123 South Broad Street, Box 227
Mankato, MN USA 56002
Web site: www.weigl.com
Copyright ©2003 WEIGL PUBLISHERS INC.
All rights reserved. No part of this publication may be reproduced, stored in a retrieval system, or transmitted in any form or by any means, electronic, mechanical, photocopying, recording, or otherwise, without the prior written permission of the publisher.

Library of Congress Cataloging-in-Publication Data

Bocknek, Jonathan.
  Stars / Jonathan Bocknek.
     v. cm. -- (Science matters)
Includes index.
Contents: Getting to know stars -- Our closest star -- Starry nights -- Star patterns -- A constellation map -- Groupings of stars -- A star is born -- Studying stars -- Surfing our solar system -- Science in action -- What have you learned?
  ISBN 1-59036-087-7 (lib. bdg. : alk. paper)
 1. Stars--Juvenile literature. [1. Stars.] I. Title. II. Series.
  QB801.7 .B63 2003
  523.8--dc21
                                   2002013854

Printed in the United States of America
1 2 3 4 5 6 7 8 9 0   06 05 04 03 02

Project Coordinator Jennifer Nault **Design** Terry Paulhus
Copy Editor Tina Schwartzenberger **Layout** Bryan Pezzi
Photo Researcher Tina Schwartzenberger

Photograph Credits
Every reasonable effort has been made to trace ownership and to obtain permission to reprint copyright material. The publishers would be pleased to have any errors or omissions brought to their attention so that they may be corrected in subsequent printings.

Cover: Galaxy from Comstock, Inc.
Bettmann/CORBIS/MAGMA: page 19; Warren Clark: page 10; COMSTOCK, Inc.: pages 1, 3B, 4, 9, 22T; Corel Corporation: pages 3T, 23T; Digital Vision: pages 3M, 6, 7, 14, 15L, 15R, 16, 23M, 23B; NASA: page 8; National Optical Astronomy Observatory/Association of Universities for Research in Astronomy/National Science Foundation: page 18; Bryan Pezzi: pages 13, 17, 21; PhotoDisc, Inc.: page 22B; Roger Ressmeyer/CORBIS/MAGMA: page 11.

Contents

Studying Stars 4

Earth's Closest Star 6

Starry Nights 8

Star Patterns 10

Star Map 12

Groups of Stars 14

A Star is Born 16

Seeing Stars 18

Surfing Our Solar System 20

Science in Action 21

What Have You Learned? 22

Words to Know/Index 24

Studying Stars

The night sky is dotted with tiny, twinkling stars. They look like specks of light in the distance. All stars appear small from Earth because they are so far away. In fact, stars are very large. Did you know that the Sun is also a star? Some stars are larger than the Sun. Others are smaller than the Sun. The **mass** of some stars can be about 10 times greater than the Sun.

■ People can see stars in the sky because of the light energy the stars produce.

Star Facts

Did you know that the Sun produces enough energy to power the United States? One second of the Sun's energy could provide power to the United States for 4 million years.

- Stars burn for billions of years.

- The Sun is a star. It is the closest star to Earth.

- After the Sun, the next nearest star to Earth is called Proxima Centauri.

- The smallest **white dwarf** stars are the same size as Earth.

- Ocean sailors once used stars to guide their way.

- A star's brightness is called luminosity.

Earth's Closest Star

Earth is about 93 million miles (150 million km) from the Sun. The Sun is the only star whose heat reaches our planet. Sunlight takes slightly more than 8 minutes to reach Earth. Light from the other stars takes much longer to reach Earth. This is because all of the other stars are much farther away.

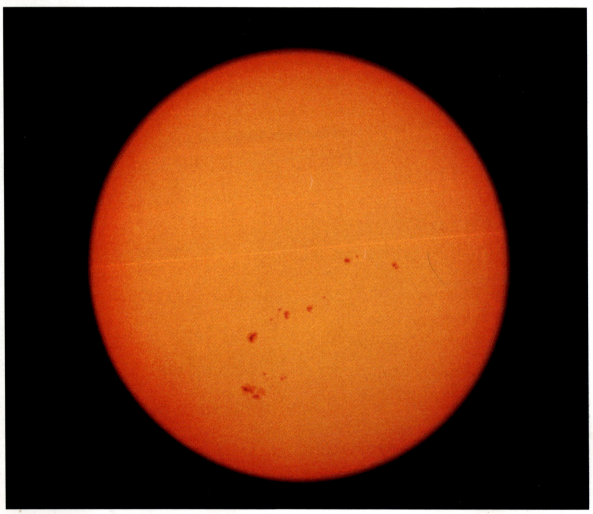

■ Earth receives the heat of the Sun. Without the Sun's heat, Earth would be cold, dark, and lifeless.

Supernovas in the Sky

Very large stars are called supergiants. Supergiants eventually die out. When they die, they explode in a fiery blaze. This explosion is called a supernova.

Supernovas can be bright enough to see from Earth. In the year 1054, people from all over the world saw a bright light in the sky. The light shone for 23 days. The supernova could be seen during the day.

Starry Nights

Stars are huge, glowing balls of swirling gases. One of these gases is called **hydrogen**. Stars are so hot that the hydrogen gas breaks apart. The heat causes hydrogen to change into **helium**. The change produces a large amount of energy. Some of the energy takes the form of heat. Some of the energy takes the form of **light**.

- Scientists measure the size of stars by studying their brightness and temperature.

Star Colors

Stars are one of three different colors. Some stars are yellow. For instance, the Sun is a yellow star. Other types of stars are blue or red.

A star's heat affects the color that can be seen from Earth. Imagine a burning candle. The blue part of the flame is the hottest part. The yellow part is less hot. The red part of the flame is the coolest.

Which type of stars do you think are hottest: red or blue?

Answer: Blue stars

Star Patterns

More than one thousand stars can be seen on a very dark night. People in ancient times saw patterns when they looked up at the twinkling stars. They imagined lines that connected the stars. These lines formed shapes. Some star shapes looked like animals, such as bears or dogs. Other star shapes formed gods or goddesses. Star patterns are called constellations.

■ Ursa Major (bottom) is called the Great Bear. Ursa Minor (top) is called the Lesser Bear.

Star Shapes

Did you know that the northern half of Earth sees a different part of the sky than the southern half? This means that the two halves of the world see different constellations in the night sky.

Constellations were created long ago. People in different parts of the world saw figures in the stars. They saw different shapes in the same star groups. Different shapes were seen in the Big Dipper. People in China saw a carriage pulled by horses. People in Mexico saw a parrot. Native Peoples in North America saw hunters chasing a bear.

The Big Dipper is shown below. What shape do you see?

Star Map

There are eighty-eight different constellations in the northern sky. Some constellations are high in the sky. They are visible all year long. Other constellations are lower in the sky. They are visible only during certain seasons. This star map and chart show the largest northern constellations.

Constellation	Meaning of Name
Andromeda	Princess
Auriga	Chariot Driver
Bootes	Shepherd
Cassiopeia	Wife of Cepheus
Cepheus	Royal Husband of Cassiopeia
Corona Borealis	Northern Crown
Cygnus	Swan
Draco	Dragon
Gemini	Twins
Hercules	Warrior
Leo	Lion
Leo Minor	Lion Cub
Lyra	Small Harp
Pegasus	Winged Horse
Perseus	Hero
Taurus	Bull
Triangulum	Triangle
Ursa Major	Great Bear
Ursa Minor	Lesser Bear
Vulpecula	Fox

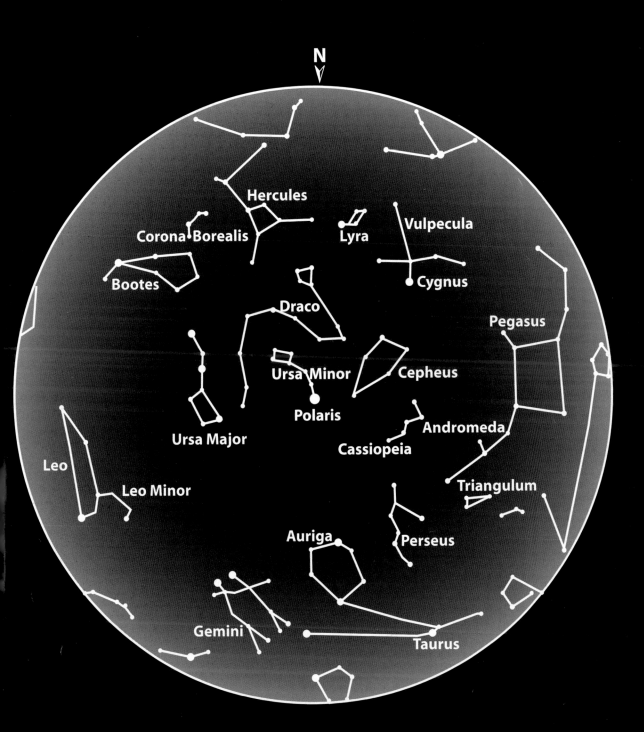

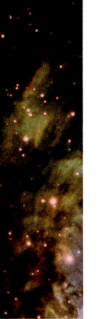

Groups of Stars

The Sun is just one of the stars that make up the Milky Way galaxy. A galaxy is a group of millions or billions of stars. The stars in a galaxy appear to be close together. They are actually very far apart from each other. There is a great deal of empty space in a galaxy.

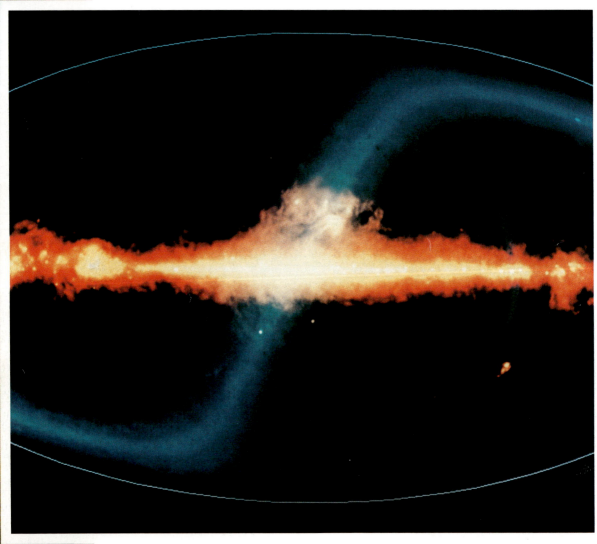

■ The Milky Way galaxy looks like a long band stretching across the sky.

Galaxy Shapes

Did you know that there are 100 billion galaxies in space? Read on to find out about the different types of galaxies.

Most galaxies are shaped like eggs in their shells. They are called elliptical galaxies. Spiral galaxies are shaped like fried eggs. The Milky Way galaxy is a spiral galaxy. A few galaxies do not have a regular shape. They are called irregular galaxies.

Spiral Galaxy

A Star is Born

Stars are born in nebulas. Nebulas are gigantic clouds of gas and dust. Most of the gas in a nebula is hydrogen. Hydrogen forms new stars. Stars use up all of their hydrogen over time. They grow dimmer and cooler as they use up their hydrogen. They stop glowing, fade out, and die.

■ The Rosette Nebula looks like a red rose in the night sky.

A Star's Life

The length of a star's life depends on the amount of gas it contains. Stars with less gas have longer lives. This is because they burn slowly.

Life Cycle of a Star

1. Dust and gas gather together. This is called a nebula.

2. A star forms.

3. The star grows, cools, and becomes red. This is called a red giant.

4. The star begins to shrink, losing its outer layers. This is called a white dwarf.

5. The star shrinks and cools until it fades away. This is called a black dwarf.

Seeing Stars

Astronomers study stars in many ways. They use different kinds of **telescopes** to see distant stars. Astronomers also use special cameras to photograph stars. They study the photographs to find changes in the stars. This is done by comparing several photographs taken over long periods of time.

Astronomers also send **space probes** into space. Space probes collect information about stars.

■ Most astronomers work in observatories. These buildings have large telescopes.

A Life of Science

Edwin Hubble

Edwin Hubble loved to read stories about space travelers when he was young. He became an astronomer when he grew up.

Edwin Hubble was the first astronomer to discover stars outside of the Milky Way galaxy. Edwin made other important discoveries about stars and the universe. The *Hubble Space Telescope* is named after Edwin.

Surfing Our Solar System

How can I find more information about space?
- Libraries have many interesting books about space.
- Science centers are great places to learn about space.
- The Internet offers some great Web sites dedicated to space.

Where can I find a good reference Web site to learn more about space?
Encarta Homepage
www.encarta.com
- Type any space-related term into the search engine. Some terms to try include "supernova" and "galaxy."

How can I find out more about space, rockets, and astronauts?
NASA Kids
http://kids.msfc.nasa.gov
- This Web site offers puzzles and games, along with the latest news on NASA's research.

Science in Action

Keep a Star Journal

Watch the stars for 1 month. Try to find the same stars every night. Are they always in the same place? Do they move across the sky? What questions do you have about the stars? Keep a journal to record your observations.

Caution: It is safe to look at all of the stars except for the Sun. Never look directly at the Sun. You can damage your eyes.

Create a Constellation

Cut many small circles out of colored paper. Glue the circles all over a piece of black or dark blue paper. Do any of the stars form a pattern? If so, you may have found your own constellation. Create a name for your constellation. See how many constellations you can find.

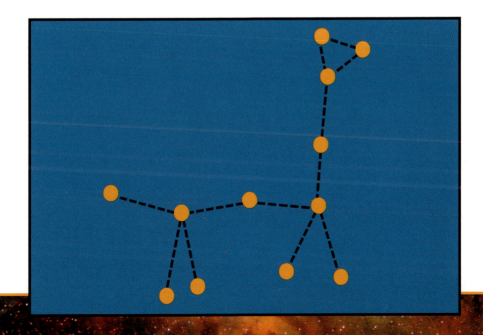

What Have You Learned?

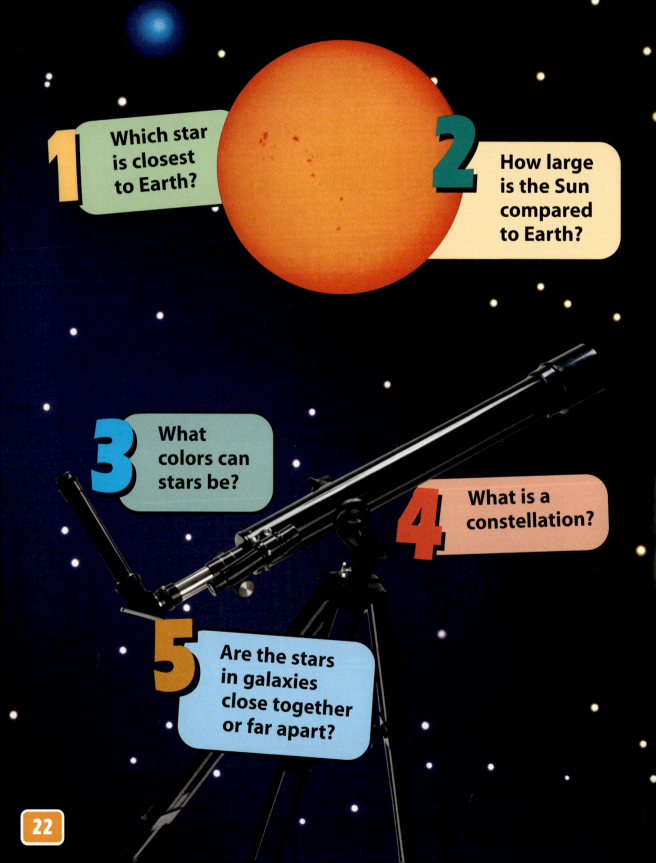

1. Which star is closest to Earth?

2. How large is the Sun compared to Earth?

3. What colors can stars be?

4. What is a constellation?

5. Are the stars in galaxies close together or far apart?

6 What shape is the Milky Way galaxy?

7 Where are stars born?

8 What happens when a star dies?

9 How bright is a supernova?

10 How do astronomers study stars?

Answers: 1. The Sun **2.** One million Earths could fit inside the Sun. **3.** Red, blue, or yellow **4.** An imaginary star pattern **5.** Far apart **6.** Spiral **7.** In nebulas **8.** It gets dimmer and cooler. **9.** A supernova is bright enough to be seen in the day. **10.** Using telescopes, cameras, or space probes

Words to Know

astronomers: people who study and teach about the planets, stars, and other objects in space

helium: a very light gas

hydrogen: a light, clear gas that burns easily

light: the form of energy that makes it possible for us to see

mass: size or bulk

space probes: spacecrafts used to gather information about space

telescopes: instruments that makes distant objects appear closer

white dwarf: a small, dim star that is hot and white

Index

Big Dipper 10, 11

color 9
constellations 10, 11, 12, 13

Earth 5, 6, 7, 8, 9, 11
energy 4, 5

galaxies 14, 15, 19

Hubble, Edwin 19
Hubble Space Telescope 19
hydrogen 4, 16

life cycle 17
light 4, 6, 7, 8
Little Dipper 10

Milky Way 14, 15, 19

nebulas 16, 17

Sun 5, 6, 8, 9, 14, 16
supergiants 7, 8
supernovas 7

telescopes 18, 19